YOU SHOULD BE SO LUCKY

and other stories

YOU SHOULD BE SO LUCKY

AND OTHER STORIES

Peter Dawson

Published by Peter Dawson
30 Elm Street
Borrowash
Derby, DE72 3HP

Cover image: Nana_studio via Adobe Stock

British Library Cataloguing-in-Publication data
A catalogue record for this book is available from the
British Library

ISBN 978-1-8383404-4-5

Typeset by Carnegie Book Production, Lancaster
Printed and bound by Jellyfish Solutions Ltd

CONTENTS

ABOUT THE AUTHOR

A graduate of the LSE, a career in teaching reached its climax with ten years as headmaster of an Inner London comprehensive school for two thousand boys and girls.

Having survived that exhilarating experience, my subsequent career was in education politics, in the Ofsted inspectorate, as a UK delegate to the EC in Brussels and finally as a lay member of the Employment Appeal tribunal in London.

During the foregoing, my books on education were published by Blackwell of Oxford. They were followed by books on employment law and on preaching by other publishers, the latter the outcome of my becoming an ordained Minister of the Methodist Church.

After retirement, my writing has been devoted to books of short stories, published for me by Scotforth Books of Lancaster. No one first venturing into the world of fiction could find a more helpful publisher, or one more committed to producing work of the highest possible standard.

All things are possible to those who believe

Jesus Christ

YOU SHOULD BE SO LUCKY

Shortly after completing the following story, the present author began reading Alan Bennett's diaries, entitled Keeping On Keeping On. *Described by one reviewer as a masterpiece of reminiscence, the introduction concludes with Bennett's belief about his life: 'It has been alright. I have been very lucky.'*

Jake Rigby believed himself to have been born lucky. 'Some folks are born lucky and some born unlucky. It just depends.' He did not explain what it depended on. He was not a deep thinker but knew what he believed.

Jake drove an old banger of a car. Some of the parts under the bonnet were tied together with string. Jake was a highly trained engineer with a first from Imperial College, London University's foremost school of engineering, so he knew exactly what to do to keep his ancient Austin Seven on the road. Friends to whom he offered lifts had one thing in common: they never accepted the offer twice. 'It's terrifying', said one, 'How that vehicle doesn't fall apart is a mystery. It's amazing he hasn't been stopped and put off the road.' Jake knew what people said. It didn't worry him. He knew he was just naturally lucky.

Jake's girl friend Isobel did not share what she saw as his buccaneering attitude. She refused to ride in his car. 'One day your luck will run out', she told him. And some said it did. Descending a steep drop in a road in heavy rain, Jake braked hard and the car aquaplaned into a wall at the bottom. The fragile old vehicle was a write-off and Jake, in a car with nothing but rattling parts and string in front of the driver to protect him, lost both his legs.

A long time afterwards, sitting in a wheelchair, Jake cheerily announced, 'It's lucky I didn't bash my brains out.' 'He wasn't born with any', said one of his friends at the pub. Jake had plenty of money and invested in a new wheelchair with more special features than a top-of-the range Mercedes. With practice, he got it up to twenty miles an hour. 'He's more dangerous in that wheelchair than he was in that old car. Watch out, everybody.'

Jake's philosophy of life had not changed with his accident. He still believed himself to be born lucky. His conviction was enhanced by the way people now treated him, giving way to him when he was driving his new machine and being helpful to him in getting him through doors and in accommodating him in his wheelchair in shops and restaurants. He said, 'All I have to do is look helpless and folk rush to my aid. Born lucky, that's me.'

Jake had an uncle, Jonathan Strong, who was Professor of Philosophy at a university. He explained Jake's view of life in terms of life in the ancient Greek city of Sparta. At a certain age, and after survival training, a boy would be taken out into the hills and left for several weeks to look after himself. He was expected to build a shelter, make and maintain a fire for cooking and keeping wild animals away, forage for food and keep himself in good condition.

It was a tough initiation. A critical preparation for this endurance test was teaching a boy that, even if events turned against him, for example, if there was a day when he could find no food, he should regard that not as a disaster but an opportunity to strengthen his fortitude. Professor Strong would tell his students, 'As with the song we sometimes hear today: always look on the bright side of life.'

Jake's uncle reckoned that Jake would have been at home in ancient Sparta. He said of his nephew, 'He's a spartan. Not even losing his legs has dampened his belief in his being born lucky. Now, I hear, he is getting interested in disabled racing, something he would not have been qualified to do before. When does this man's belief in looking on the bright side end?'

Jake had taken to going to watch paraplegic athletics. He saw many amazing performances, none more remarkable than a pole-vaulter, with one good and one false leg, who was able to clear twenty-five feet. But what really took his attention was legless racers in adapted vehicles hurtling round an athletics track. 'I'm going to have a go at that', he thought. His mind was made up when he watched the Paralympics on television and saw what was possible. He told his friends at the pub, who were dubious about his new-found interest in racing, 'If that amazing girl who's been made a dame can do it, so can I.'

Jake invested in a vehicle specially designed for racing and was soon taking part in competitions. It was not long before he came first in a race and got his name in the paper. 'See how lucky I am!' he told his mates at the Red Lion. He triumphantly asserted: 'None of you has got a cup on his sideboard for winning a race.'

Isobel had remained Jake's girl friend, though no more, throughout the vicissitudes of his life. She had come not only to care for him but to admire him. 'I don't know how you do it', she would say to him, 'I get miserable and feel life's unbearable if my washing machine breaks down. Looking on the bright side takes a lot of training.' His reply was typical of the man: 'Yes, but it's easier if you believe you are born lucky. I guess it's what you believe that matters in this life.'

ASPECTS OF FAMILY LIFE

Jake said: 'My parents tell me they care about me but all they do is tell me off.' His friend Dixie responded: 'Mine are the same. It's just that they are scared we will end up out of control and people will say it's because of poor parenting; because of the way we've been brung up. It's like when Plummy says in his posh voice when we've been playing him up: you boys are really too *challenging*.' Dixie's imitation of Mr Plumpton, their English teacher, had Jake laughing. He said, 'You're right. Our parents find us challenging. Perhaps it would have been easier for them if we'd been girls.' 'Don't you believe it,' said Dixie, 'Girls can be a right pain. Think of that Rosie Buxton. She's a right tearaway.' 'But she's a nice shape', said Jake who, coming up to fourteen, had just begun to notice such things.

'I'll tell you what', said Jake, 'I get on ever so well with my gran. We have lovely chats. She listens to me as if I'm worth listening to and tells me all sorts of interesting things. Remember when I got into trouble in PE when we were playing football and I brought down Harry Wilson with a hard tackle?

Mr Webb was furious. He said I could have broken Wilson's leg. He said I was trying to be a hard man like that Arsenal defender they call Biteyerlegs Bailey.'

He went on: 'Me and dad go to Arsenal when they're at home but I didn't dare to tell him what Webby had said about me. But I told gran. She didn't tell me off. She said, "Did you say sorry to the boy you knocked over? You should, you know. That would put things right." So I did, And do you know what? He laughed and said Webby had made too much fuss about it. Then he gave me a toffee. How about that!'

Jake's gran Marjorie sat opposite her husband Frank at breakfast. He was behind his newspaper but she didn't mind. She could enjoy her breakfast rather than listen to her husband's endless complaints about the government. He and his mates at the bowls club reckoned they ought to be running the country. Suddenly, Frank said, 'Hey, Marje, listen to this. The Archbishop of Canterbury has read out, in the House of Lords, a piece written by an eight-year-old boy about grandmothers:

A grandmother is a lady who has no children of her own, so she likes other people's little girls and boys. A grandfather is a man grandmother. He goes for walks with the boys and they talk about fishing and tractors.

Grandmothers don't have to do anything but be there. They are old, so they shouldn't play hard or run. Usually they are fat, but not too fat to tie children's shoes.

They wear glasses and funny underwear, and they can take their teeth and gums off. They don't have to be smart, only answer questions like why dogs hate cats and why God isn't married. They don't talk baby talk like visitors. When they read to us, they don't skip bits or mind if it is the same story over again. Everybody should have one, especially if they don't have television, because grandmothers are the only grown-ups who have time.

Jake's gran laughed then said, 'You know, there's some truth in that. Our Jane and her Joe spend an awful lot of time at work. Jake says they are so stressed out that all they're up for at home is telling him off.'

Joe was a supermarket manager. He claimed that his life was dominated by sales figures. He often said, 'That's capitalism for you. If you don't sell, you don't survive.' A keen theatregoer, he thought Arthur Miller's *Death of a Salesman* was one of the most powerful plays ever written. He said, 'Sometimes I know just how Willy Loman felt when he couldn't sell his stuff any more.'

Joe's wife Jane was a solicitor, specializing in immigration issues. She spent her days representing asylum seekers to officialdom. It was a frustrating task, requiring her often to be available long after normal working hours. She skipped meals and took medication for her nerves. Her doctor had told her to slow down, but she told him: 'How can I? These people are desperate.' A close friend had once told her, 'I wonder how you ever had time to have a baby.' 'Me too', she replied, 'and I do worry about Jake. He's a problem. But his gran is good with him.'

Jake's friend Dixie had a different kind of home. His father was a plumber and his mother only worked part-time at a bakery. He had three siblings and the house was sometimes in uproar when they were all having a lively time. When they got told off, it didn't bother them. When Kate, their mother, said she would get their father to deal with them when he came home, they smiled at one another. It was a hollow threat. Bill was a real softie about his kids and would simply wink at them and tell them to behave.

'Why do your parents call you Dixie?', asked Jake. 'Well', came the reply, 'they used to call me Richard, a bit posh like, which upset me a bit. When I was ten, I was worried about what would happen when you and me went to the comprehensive. Would they laugh at me for being a toff? My parents worked out that I was anxious about something so I said I didn't like being Richard. I explained that I would rather be Dick, see. They laughed and after that, I was Dixie. They didn't mind. I know they care about me and want me to be happy.'

Clive Wright, the Headmaster of the comprehensive school, saw family life as the key to a young person's success. 'Nine times after ten', he would say, 'if a boy or girl is a problem in school, it's down to the situation at home. Parents who have time for the children they have created rarely have problems with them. Sometimes a youngster has a better relationship with a grandparent than those at home.'

Jake and Dixie stood in front of the Headmaster with heads bowed. They had been sent by their physics teacher for fooling about with the gas taps in the science lab during a lesson. The teacher was a newcomer to the staff, just out of college, and scared of blowing the place up in his second week.

'Very dangerous', said the Headmaster to the boys, 'Must I send for your parents to come and see me about your behaviour?' Dixie thought his dad would be scared to come. Jake thought, 'They won't be able to come. They're too busy.' In the end the boys were let off with a reprimand. The Headmaster sought the new physics teacher at break and congratulated him on taking a firm line at the start of his career at the school. John Stuckey, the young man in question, went off for his break time coffee with a song in his heart.

Once a year, the Headmaster addressed a conference of social workers, probation officers, members of the police and people working with the young in the caring and nursing professions on the subject of sex education. He stressed the importance of ensuring that young people properly understood human sexuality, rather than depending on its salacious presentation in the media. That always brought murmurs of approval from his audience, but the subject of sex education was simply the Headmaster's device for driving home the need for all adults to realize the critical importance of the extended family in the upbringing of the young.

The conference was held in a large room in the maternity department of a London hospital. One year, the Headmaster was amused to see a poster with a warning to young nurses handling child birth. The poster said: REMEMBER THE FIRST FEW HOURS OF LIFE ARE DANGEROUS. A wag had added in black felt tip: THE LAST FEW HOURS ARE PRETTY DODGY TOO.

Clive Wright quoted the poster in his presentation to make the point that any hour in a teenager's life might be one when something said might change their lives. 'Be careful what you say to young people', he insisted, 'be it in anger, or perhaps quite casually. It may be the most important thing they hear that day, that week, for their whole lives. They may remember your words forever.' A probation officer in the audience, known for his irritability, shifted uneasily in his seat.

Jake and Dixie entered the sixth form at school together. They were now quite seriously interested in girls. In a General Studies lesson, the subject of marriage came up when they were following a course entitled the Elements of Social Structure. Afterwards, Jake said to his friend, 'I'm not getting married. The thought of trying to bring up kids puts me right off.' 'Oh, I dunno', responded Dixie, 'we had a great time at home with four of us.' In the lesson, the teacher had said, 'Your own experience will powerfully affect how you feel about family life.'

BLUE MURDER

This is not a murder mystery. There is not much mystery about it. Readers will probably work out what is going on quite early in the story. The question is, how long will it take the police?

The woman's body lay on its back. There was a bullet hole right between her eyes, found when a carefully cut rectangle of blue silk material draped over her face was removed. 'Oh Gawd', said Detective Sergeant Bucksey, 'we've got another nut case like that BA pilot a couple of years ago.'

Two years before, it had taken too long to catch a killer who left the same marker at each scene. Clutched in the hand of the victim, invariably a British Airways flight steward, would be a page torn from a BA schedule of flights. The killer had been a pilot with a grievance against BA for sacking him for being drunk in charge of an aircraft. Colleagues he had flown with had shown no sympathy because he had more than once been drinking before take off. After his arrest, he said to Detective Inspector

Coker, 'You should have caught me before. I left you the same clue every time.' 'The bastard wanted to be caught', said the DI to Bucksey.

The young woman whose body now lay before DI Coker and DS Bucksey was the second victim to have been left with a piece of blue silk on her face. The pathologist confirmed that she had been shot at close range by a gun with a silencer. Like the first victim, she had been on her way home after being in the audience at a concert performance at the Royal Festival Hall in London.

DI Keith Coker and his wife Jane were concert-goers. Their friend Paul Stone often took them with him to hear his wife, Sonia Senniston, a soprano of international repute. 'What's it like,' Jane Coker once asked Paul, 'for a futures trader to be married to a famous soprano?' 'Tempestuous' he replied. 'I guess it's her temperament that makes her such a brilliant performer, but she needs careful handling at home. Her fury when she feels she has sung badly explains why we have a crockery shortage.' Jane and her husband laughed uproariously. Paul Stone added: 'I know she finds me a dull old stick these days. When we first met, I was a war hero.'

'Your wife has a wonderful voice', said Keith, 'and looks stunning in that fabulous blue dress.' 'Yes', said Paul proudly, 'it's my favourite. She cannot wear it if she is playing a part in costume but she wears it when she is doing a solo performance at the Royal

Festival Hall with John Wilson's orchestra. She says he is the most fun conductor she has ever worked with.' He shook his head. 'She tells me that when she has found me particularly boring.'

Back at the incident room at the police station, the DI and his DS looked at the display they were building up following two murders. 'So here', said the DI, 'we have a killer who knows how to use a gun and victims who are both woman on their way home from concerts. What about that piece of material on her face. Significant?' 'Dunno', replied Bucksey, 'but I bet it means something'.

The relationship between Paul Stone and his wife deteriorated. It was not all that surprising. As a trader on the stock exchange, his life was spent calculating the likely movement of shares in the futures market. Guessing the future was the name of the game and he found it exciting. It fascinated Paul but it made him a dull companion for a lively singing star. After seven years of marriage, Sonia found herself saying repeatedly to her husband, 'Paul, you are one of the most boring people on God's earth.' As her career began to take a downward turn, with fewer invitations to perform, she became frustrated and tetchy. The crockery on the kitchen dresser steadily diminished.

Paul's life had once been more exciting. As a young man required to do national service in the military for two years, which he chose to extend, he had been commissioned in the Sussex Light Infantry. Posted to serve in the Korean War, he led his men with distinction and was mentioned in despatches. He became an expert marksman with rifle and pistol.

On a spell of leave before being demobilized, he booked a room in a London hotel and looked round for ways of enjoying himself after the horrors of Korea. Still in uniform, he went to the Palace Theatre one evening to a performance of *Oklahoma*. He was mesmerized by the girl playing the female lead.

Having learned in the military the importance of initiative, Paul went round to the stage door and waited for Sonia Senniston to emerge. He congratulated her one her performance and invited her out for a drink. She was impressed by the ribbons on his chest but said, 'Why should I drink with you? Are you someone special?' He replied, 'I'm just back from a war zone with some great tales to tell. I've been saving our nation. I promise not to bore you.' And he didn't.

His stories of heroic escapades in Korean terrain had Sonia, in her early twenties and still girlishly frisky, bouncing up and down on her chair in the *Queen's Head* on Charing Cross Road. 'I shot him right between the eyes at twenty yards', he said, concluding an account of being faced by an enemy in a barren landscape.

'He's got to be a killer who knows how to use a pistol', said DI Coker to DS Bucksey, 'That shot between her eyes was that of a marksman. Check up the records on any of our known villains who is a top shot. And take that latest piece of silk round shops that might have sold it. It looks expensive so you know where to go. Bond Street would be good place to start. Take that new Detective Constable with you to share the load. DC Acland seems a bright lad.'

Sonia decided she had had enough of her husband Paul. She screamed at him that she was leaving before he melted her brains with his boring talk and destroyed her libido with his pathetic performance in bed. He winced. His wife swept round the house, collecting the clothes and other items she wanted. She laughed cruelly as she tossed her blue silk dress at him. 'Here you are, you lifeless lump of lard,' she shouted, 'wrap that round you in bed to make you feel like a man.'

DS Bucksey found what he was after in a dress shop in Mayfair, he and his young companion having given up on Bond Street. 'Oh yes', said the obsequious attendant at Penry's Mayfair Boudoir, after he had looked up his records. 'We made a dress of this material for one of our most famous customers, the soprano Sonia Senniston. We make all her dresses, and her lingerie as well. She is very fussy about it. She says she must be glamorous all through.' 'Should we look at some lingerie', whispered the DC hopefully. 'Keep your mind on the job in hand or you will be back on the beat tomorrow', replied Bucksey.

Paul Stone asked Keith Coker how his attempts to catch the blue silk killer was going. The DI thought to himself that it was just the opportunity he needed. He said, 'Why not come to the incident room and see?' Paul was surprised and uneasy when he saw his picture among those of suspects on the incident display board. Seated across a table from Paul, the DI asked, 'How is Sonia these days?' 'She's left me', came the terse reply. 'Really?', responded Coker, 'and taken all her clothes with her?' Sonia Senniston's husband thought that was an odd question. He remained silent. 'You haven't been cutting up that blue silk dress, have you?' asked Coker.

So Paul Stone's murderous activities came to an end. Under interrogation, he admitted that his fury at his wife's departure, and the style of it, had led him to be revenged on women attending music concerts. 'I know it wasn't the thing to do, but there you go.' The killer spoke as if talking about stealing an apple from a greengrocer's display. 'I guess I wanted you to catch me', said the prisoner, 'after all, I left you some helpful clues, didn't I?' 'We've heard that one before', said the DI angrily.

There was a darkly dramatic end to the story. Preparing to interview Stone before sentencing, a psychiatrist had gone to the trouble of researching the man's military record. He discovered that his service in Korea had not been the uninterrupted catalogue of heroic deeds he pretended. In captivity with the enemy for six months before escaping, he had suffered intense interrogation that caused great damage. He had spent some time in a military facility for men suffering from stress disorders after combat, the most affected of whom displayed bizarre behaviour. Captain Stone's unpredictably violent conduct, falling not short of menacing people's lives when thwarted in any way, led to his eventual discharge from the army. The military authorities neglected to warn the civilian population of the man they were letting loose on them.

'It turns out', declared the psychiatrist, 'that the man is mentally damaged. Not to put too fine a point on it, he's slightly mad. His wife was lucky to survive. He could still be dangerous.' So, unsurprisingly, Paul Stone ended up in Broadmoor, a prison for the criminally insane. He was perfectly happy there, endlessly playing records of his wife singing.

THE BEST NIGHT
OF THE WEEK

'I was one, you know', said Julie, 'and so were you'. She was addressing her friend Jackie. The proprietor of the coffee shop where the two women were talking had put on an old tape of ABBA singing *Dancing Queen.* Jackie said, 'We were down the Trocadero of a Saturday night with the others. Friday night we washed our hair and got our kit ready for Saturday. After work Saturday came the best night of the week. We came alive at the Troc with ABBA telling us girls we were dancing queens.' 'We believed it, you know', said her friend. She paused. Now in her sixties, she looked back across the years, then added, 'For those few hours on a Saturday, our lives had new meaning after the boring, boring days at work in the week. We were ...' She hesitated, searching for the right word to describe the experience. 'We were *uplifted*', she said, with just a hint of a catch in her throat as she relived days long gone.

The two women, who met every few weeks for a bite and a chat at a coffee shop, had been at school together and such close friends that they were known among their contemporaries as JJ. Julie and Jackie were inseparable in their teens. Forty years on, they enjoyed reminiscing about the days when they were still wondering how their lives might turn out.

Both had successful marriages and all but one of their children had grown up to be pleasant and caring people. Sadly, Julie had a son who died of meningitis in infancy, which cast a dark shadow across her life, and that of her family. But they had come to terms with their loss after a period of great sadness. Julie had been helped by a counsellor who told her: 'We all have to face up to the fact that there are tears in life. We can't get from the cradle to the grave without having to deal with occasional heartbreak. Give it time and the sun will come out again.'

At one stage, Jackie's marriage was in trouble. Her husband Matt came to her one day – she would never forget it – to say he had been unfaithful. He insisted on explaining that he had had a one-night stand with a young woman he had met when away in Norway, negotiating a deal in his medical equipment business. His exchanges with a hospital consortium had produced a deal worth half a million and he was ecstatic. When a Norwegian beauty, there to record decisions on behalf of one hospital in the consortium, made eyes at him over drinks after the deal was sealed, he was in a mood to celebrate. As they say, one thing led to another.

'Why are you telling me all this?' screamed Jackie, 'I don't want to hear the sordid details of your disgusting behaviour. I suppose you are going to tell me you are leaving me. Go on then. Clear off back to Norway. I hope the cold winters freeze your balls off.'

Matt winced. 'Look', he said, 'I'm devoted to you. You're the only woman I have ever cared about. I was so ashamed of what happened that I decided to confess and ask for forgiveness. Please, please forgive me.' By the time Matt had finished this little speech, Jackie had calmed down. 'I'll think about it' she said. 'Go and book a table to take me out to dinner. We must *properly* celebrate the deal you made in Norway.' She emphasized the word properly.

JJ shared all the goings-on in their lives and Julie assured her friend that she had dealt with her wayward husband in just the right way. She insisted, 'Men are easily led into temptation. Whoever created the poor things gave them a massive sex drive in order to maintain the population. You know, the Bible says God promised Abraham his descendants would be more numerous than the dust of the earth. A man's first duty, it was believed, was to procreate as often as possible.' 'Thank heavens those days are gone' said Jackie, 'but the drive is still there in some men'. Laughing, Julie said, 'And it's sometimes our job to snuff it out.' Then she added, still laughing, 'But only sometimes!'

The ABBA tape was still playing in the coffee shop. After the marriages of the four members of ABBA to one another had failed, they recorded a sadly poignant song entitled *The Winner Takes It All*. They had assured the media it was not auto-biographical but it touched the hearts of ABBA followers whose relationships had not endured.

As the song pulsated while JJ drank their coffee, Julie said, 'Have you heard their new CD marking forty years on? It's called *Voyage*. Joe bought it for me. He said being married to a dancing queen had been a wonderful voyage, even when it was a bit stormy.'

'What are the new songs like? Does ABBA sound the same?' asked Jackie. 'No', came the reply, 'their singing is no longer that of a bunch of young pop singers. The sound is deeper and more mature, as you would expect. But the girl's voices still blend beautifully and they are still ABBA. As for the songs, they're no longer ring-a-ding but echo the experiences of a lifetime.'

'For example?' inquired Jackie. 'Well', said her friend Julie, 'one song is called *I Can be That Woman* and is a sort of yearning song about what might have been. The closing lines have stayed with me:

You're not the man you should've been
I let you down somehow
I'm not the woman I could've been
But I can be that woman now

Julie went on: 'Joe said that's been us at times, like with every couple who have ever believed they belonged together. He really spoke from the heart about it. He said that song is very profound and quite moving. My Joe is not a sentimental bloke', mused Julie, 'but he has deep feelings that don't often show. I mean, for heaven's sake, he's a football manager. It's a blood and guts job. He can't let his feelings show.'

'He nearly did last week', said Jackie, smiling, 'when Rangers lost in that penalty shoot-out. I thought he was going to punch that TV interviewer on the nose when he suggested Joe might face the sack if Rangers didn't do better.' 'I wish he had', said Julie, 'it would have livened things up after a very boring match. You know, I can't stand football. I only go so I know what Joe has to put up with. They spent a lot of money on that new striker and Joe says he couldn't hit a barn door at six paces.'

'It's a good job we wives are around to offer our men TLC', said Jackie, 'the poor things wouldn't survive otherwise. I guess that's what marriage is about a good deal of the time – a sort of survival kit in face of the world's hardships.' 'Yes', came

Julie's response, 'and mostly, the longer it lasts, the stronger it gets.'

'Just look at us', said Jackie, 'a couple of old dancing queen's talking about the meaning of life.' She paused, then declared, 'I suppose we have to thank ABBA for that.'

BECOMING A HERO

This story provides a good example of my way of writing, which involves the characters in a story taking over its development. When this one began, I thought it was going to be about gardening and garden centres, but it ended up being about football. That was not at all in my mind when Bert talked about his roses. Neither of us knew he was going to become a sort of football hero.

'I've got roses bloomin' in me garden and it's nearly the end of November. Never had that before', said Bert. 'It's global warming', responded his friend Harold, who always knew everything, spoke posher than Bert and would not tolerate being called Harry. 'You mean like what they call climate change?', said Bert. 'I've not paid much attention to all that stuff in the news on telly about floods and such goin's on. I only watch *East Enders.*'

'Bert', said his friend, 'you were always like that at school. Remember how old Dicky Doughnut used to tell you that you only listened when it was history.'

'Well', came the reply, 'it were exitin' hearin' about them crewsides, and what some of them kings got up to. Especially fat Henry wotsit and all them wimmin he married before doin' 'em in.' '*Crusades* not crewsides', said Harold, 'and Henry didn't do all his wives in. He sent Ann of Cleves packing when he saw how ugly she was. They called her the Dutch Mare because she had a face like a horse. Actually, she was lucky to be sent back where she came from.'

Bert grinned mischievously as he recalled days at primary school. He said, 'Remember we woz in Mr Dixon's class. He had glasses on his nose with a ribbon on one end and they fell off when he got cross and hung over his belly by the ribbon.' Harold interjected. 'The glasses were called pince nez,' he said, authoritatively.

'The whole school called Mr Dixon Dicky Doughnut', said Bert, 'I got stopped by the Headmaster in the corridor one day and he asked me which form I was in. Wivout thinkin', I said, "Mr Doughnut's". The headmaster's face turned bright red. It wasn't 'cos he was cross. He was tryin' not to laugh.'

Bert and Harold had remained close friends all their lives, although their paths had taken very different directions after primary school and the Doughnut days. Harold had made it to the grammar school and became a solicitor while Bert went to the secondary modern and ended up on the conveyor belt at the local factory turning out the Ford Fiesta.

What explained the two men's continuing friend-ship was their interest in football. Saturdays would find them on the terrace at Slingsby Wanderers, the local soccer team, whose achievements were for the most part of minor significance. The club was firmly established in the middle of the Buxley League, one of the country's many leagues in the lower echelons of the soccer world.

The Wanderers, whose players earned a living in a variety of occupations, were not fully amateur because Jack Buckmaster, who sponsored Slingsby Wanderers, paid the players fifty pounds each if they won. It added a frisson of excitement to matches and certainly gave motivation to the players. Buckmaster was a man who believed he knew how to handle people. 'You have to give them a reason for making an effort', he insisted.

Jack Buckmaster had been at primary school with Bert and Harold. He had made a great deal of money in the business of motor repairs. His belief was that, for most men and women, having their car off the road for any length of time was at best a great nuisance and at worst a disaster. He owned no fewer than seven garages and repair shops and drove a Mercedes to show the world he amounted to something. He was a large man with an ego to match. It delighted him to have two old school pals in his entourage of admirers on the Wanderers match days. His generous bonhomie in the bar after matches, especially if the Wanderers won, was the talk of the town.

Bert's wife Sybil thought he was football crazy, and told him so. On a Saturday morning, he leapt out of bed full of energy and his conversation at breakfast was entirely devoted to the Wanderer's prospects. He was critical of the manager, Harry Cook, who just did not have an eye for real talent in Bert's view. He said, 'That new player Harry recruited from the comprehensive is useless. His control of a football is about as good as the government's control of inflation. We need a proper talent spotter.'

Sybil was always glad when Bert went off to the match after lunch. Soon after, she would be away for an afternoon with other football wives doing something important like going round shops looking at clothes or shoes, or wandering off to the pictures. Susie, a lively and witty member of the group said: 'I guess we're wanderers too, like that bloody football team.'

Disaster struck one Saturday when Bert was knocked down crossing the road on the way to the match. He spent a long time in hospital and lost an eye and a leg. Sybil was distraught. She told her friends, 'Bert was always such a happy chap, what with his roses and his football, but the spirit has gone out of him. It's downright depressing at home now. He's supposed to have an artificial limb fitted but won't go.'

Talking to Harold about Bert's situation, Jack Buckmaster said, 'We need to motivate him. We need to give him a reason to get on his feet and start living again. Tell you what. Let's have him on the board at the Wanderers and give him the job of going round spotting new talent.'

Harold and Jack went to visit Bert at home. Sybil was delighted to see them but shook her head when they told her they'd come to get Bert on his feet again. 'You'll be lucky', she said, 'he's only interested in feeling sorry for himself. He says he's just a one-eyed cripple, no good for anything.' 'Leave him to us', said Jack, full of good cheer, 'we're going to make him famous in this locality.'

Both men were greeted with a warm but suspicious kind of welcome. 'Great to see you', said Bert, 'it's good of you to find time for a wreck like me.' 'Come off it', said Jack, 'we need you at the Wanderers. We've got a job for you. We want you on the board. You're just the man to become our talent spotter. You always used to moan about Harry Cook's efforts. Now's the time to show us what you can do.' 'Well', said Bert, 'I never thought I'd end up on the board at Wanderers. How about that?'

And so it came about that Bert spent his Saturday mornings visiting secondary schools and the local sixth form college and the FE college, looking for football talent in their first elevens as they played one another on Saturday mornings. He soon found he was not alone in scouting for players who might have a future in the game. Scouts from professional teams were out as well.

It was at Hadley, a nearby town, that Bert spotted James Rushton at the grammar school. At seventeen, he had that rare talent in a striker for leaving the opposition searching for him. How did he manage to be so unobtrusive? Suddenly, he would turn up in the goal area just as a lofted pass soared over everyone else to land on his head for a goal.

Bert was not surprised that a talent spotter from a professional club was there to see Rushton. He beat Bert to it and got to the player first after the match. The two had a long conversation. Bert hung around to give time for the players to change then approached Rushton when he appeared in his smart school uniform. Well, it was a grammar school. Bert said, 'You have real talent. You might have a future in this game.' With great courtesy, Rushton replied, 'Thank you, sir. I've just been told that by another gentleman.' 'Yes', said Bert, 'and you've perhaps been offered a chance to sign up for training with a professional club.' 'Yes', came the eager reply, 'but I don't know what the Headmaster will think, let alone my dad, because I'm entered for a scholarship at Cambridge.'

'Look', said Bert, 'most lads who sign up with big clubs never make it into a soccer career. If playin'' football for a livin' is what you really want, you need to start with an amachewer club like mine. Come and play for Slingsby Wanderers before you go off to Cambridge. You can play when you're there. Joinin' a professional club after you've gradulated will be no big problem if you're are as good a footballer like it looks. But get some seckurty be'ind you wiv a diggery in case your football career don't come orf.'

Jimmy Rushton was highly intelligent and thought the one-eyed man with a limp addressing him made sense, despite his way of talking. It would not have been gone uncorrected at Hadley Grammar. Leggy Barlow, head of English at the school, and so called because of his long legs, first seen in the annual staff versus boys match, would have no truck with boys who distorted the English language. 'If you cannot speak properly', he would say to any boy from a working class background with a poor command of the spoken word, 'If you cannot speak properly, it would be better if you kept quiet. But we will teach you how to utter English utterly well.'

Leggy was rather proud of this aphorism, which was amusingly repeated by boys with skills in imitating members of staff. Greg Selby of the lower fifth was wizard at it. 'We will teach you', he would say, one hand clutching each lapel as Leggy often did, 'We will teach you to utter English utterly well.' It never failed to raise a laugh as the teacher approached the class he was about to teach, where Selby was the classroom entertainer.

Jimmy Rushton became Slingsy Wanderers' leading striker before going to Cambridge. At the annual soccer match between Oxford and Cambridge, he scored a hat trick and was carried shoulder high from the pitch. But he scored even more impressively in his finals with a top first in law. Within six years of graduating, he had established a reputation in chambers in the Middle Temple in London. In due course, he took silk and was leading cases in the High Court. He became a very rich man.

'Here', said Jack Buckmaster to his guests in the bar after a Wanderers match, 'look at this.' Now somewhat grizzled in appearance, with a head of grey hair and a massive paunch, he still commanded attention. He waved a letter in the air. 'Remember Jimmy Rushton when he was our top striker? Well, he's giving us a quarter of a million. It's to say thanks to us for having him, and especially to Bert for steering him in the right direction. He says Bert is his hero. How about that?' Bert, now retired from talent spotting but still on the Wanderers board, said to his friend Harold, 'Fancy that. You know, if I hadn't lost and eye and a leg, I would never have become a hero.'

BLACK DASH

Jackson Ubango, a native of Ghana, was the fastest runner over four hundred metres ever seen at Ginley Athletics Club. He liked his nickname, Black Dash. He would joke to English club mates, 'Me Black Dash, you White Trash'. It was just banter with no racist connotations. Everybody liked Jackson.

Jackson's parents had come to England when their son was small to find a better standard of living than his father Emmanual could find in Africa. He was an intelligent man and highly conscientious in performance of any work he could find. He was a deeply religious man and, if asked about his approach to work, would say, 'I believe in Jesus. He set the standard. Scripture says that whatever the Lord gives you to do, you should do it with all your might.'

Emmanual Ubango, known as Manny, began work at Ginley railway station, near Leicester, as a station porter. Always immaculate, polite and reliable, he quickly came to the attention of the station manager who said to him, 'How about training as a signalman? We need three to provide twenty-four-hour cover and Bill Ogilvy is retiring.' So, after training, Jackson's father become a signalman.

The signal box at Ginley when he was on duty was always immaculate. He brought furniture polish and a duster to work to keep everything looking spick and span. His two colleagues laughed at him and claimed the signal box had never looked so posh. One of them said, 'It's because he thinks Jesus is watching.'

To the delight of his father, Jackson had done well at school in England and gained a place at Bristol University, where he studied languages. He secured a post teaching French at Ginley Grammar School. When first appointed, some of the staff had their doubts about an African teaching French to English boys and girls, but he turned out to be such a brilliant teacher that their doubts were soon allayed.

The esteem in which Jackson's pupils held him was advanced by his performance as an athlete. His performances representing Ginley Athletic Club at athletic events often got his name into the local paper. His name began to appear in the national press as the selection of England's team for the forthcoming Olympics became newsworthy. When Jackson was chosen for the four hundred metres, a girl at school approached him hesitantly, with her giggling friends looking on, to ask for his autograph.

At the club where Jackson trained, people began to look at him with new respect. He told his father, 'They look up to me, even if Joe Ridgewell still regards me as part of the white man's burden.' Ridgewell was a rather arrogant pole-vaulter of old-fashioned racist tendencies. Jackson's friend Roger told him, 'Ignore Ridgewell. He's up the pole. He'll fall off it half way up one of these days and break his neck.' The remark was prescient. The man in question damaged his spine in training and disappeared from the club.

A newcomer to the club made the mistake of acknowledging Ubango by saying, 'Hi there, Jack.' 'My name is Jackson', came the cool response. The newcomer asked someone nearby, 'Why is he so touchy about his name?' An elderly member of the club intervened and took the inquirer aside. 'You need', he said, 'to realize that Jackson Ubango comes from a very religious family. They worship at the Jesus Saves Evangelical Church. In his youth, Jackson's father came under the influence of a missionary preacher named Albert Jackson. That's how our famous four hundred metre runner got his name. He doesn't like it abbreviated.'

At the Olympics, Jackson faced the greatest ever test of his beliefs as he won his heat and secured a place in the semi-finals. He felt sure Jesus was near him, leading him on.

But he came second in his semi-final and realized he had probably met his match in the man who beat him, the great German runner Gustav Schmidt. As the two finished the race, they breathlessly embraced one another. The German said, 'Well done. That's the closest run I've faced for ages. But I'll get to the tape first tomorrow.'

Jackson wondered if Jesus would help him in the final. Someone sidled up to him and said, 'You'll need some help to win tomorrow.' 'Yes', replied Jackson, 'I know.' The man who had approached him held out a small packet. 'This will do it for you', he said, 'It'll cost you a couple of tenners. Just pop it in half an hour before the race and you will fly round the track.' 'Go away', said Jackson. The man shrugged. As he walked away he said, 'I'll be around if you change your mind.'

That night, Jackson lay in bed thinking of what would happen if he won the four hundred metre final. The adulation would be wonderful. Unlike his normal practice, he did not consult Jesus. His reluctance was down to his awareness that the one he regarded as his closest friend would disapprove of what he had in mind. He recalled something his friend Roger once said to him, 'You shouldn't let religion get in the way of common sense. You've got to grab the opportunities life throws your way.'

The four hundred metres final was scheduled for the afternoon of the next day. During the morning, Jackson wandered round outside the stadium, a twenty pound note burning a metaphorical hole in his pocket. He ended up in a coffee shop, moodily stirring a coffee. Suddenly, he felt the man who had approached him yesterday slip into the seat beside him. 'Good morning', he said, 'any second thoughts?'

Trying not to think about what he was doing, Jackson slid the twenty from his pocket and pushed it across the table. 'Good luck in the race', said the man as he handed over the small packet he had shown him before. 'But you won't need luck. You're bound to win.'

Jackson and Gustav Schmidt left the rest of the field trailing as they raced round the track. At the final bend, the German suddenly accelerated and made his customary sprint to the tape, but Jackson, who felt uplifted and empowered as he had never done before, went past him.

As the two embraced after the finish, Schmidt said, 'God alone knows how you did that.' Jackson thought, 'Yes, he does.' On the victory rostrum, Jackson was in tears as the UK national anthem was played. Cameras zoomed in on him and people thought his tears were ones of joy. They were not. He was filled with shame for what he had done.

The adulation he received on arriving home in Ginley unnerved him. Crowds welcomed him at the railway station; a trumpeter from the town's brass band sounded a noisy fanfare as he emerged into the street; banners were strung across the road where he lived. His muted response to all this was put down to his modesty.

A great fuss was made of him as he arrived indoors at his home. He put his hand on his father's arm and said, 'Father, I must have a private word with you.' Alone together, Jackson explained how he had given way to temptation to win his gold medal. His father did not angrily expostulate but, as was his way, said quietly, 'We must think about how you might put things right. Say nothing to anyone. By tomorrow, what you must do will have been revealed to me.'

Next day, Jackson went to his father with apprehension but confidence. Emmanuel, a man of such rectitude that anyone with a problem might go to him for advice, said: 'The Lord Jesus has made clear to me your sentence. You must go down to the river, kneel on the bank and ask God's forgiveness, then throw your gold medal into the river. You must resign from you school post and from the athletics club and go away from here for five years. All you must say by way of explanation is that it is the Lord's will. When you have done all this, you may return.' 'Thank you father', said Jackson, and fell into his father's arms, weeping.

At a time when there was a national shortage of teachers of foreign languages, Jackson found a post at a large London multi-ethnic comprehensive. It was not as easy as teaching at a grammar school but certainly more exciting. He quickly took to it and found himself exhausted but exhilarated at the end of the day.

There were three other newcomers to the staff as well as Jackson and they soon made common cause, sharing their experiences. One of the three was a pretty Welsh girl named Ceinwen and, after a couple of terms, Jackson realized he was more than a little interested in her. She had trained to teach in London at the college known as Domski which specialized in domestic science. Ceinwen taught what was called in the school's curriculum housecraft, which Jackson assumed was cooking and stuff.

Ceinwen was a small, delicate creature and Jackson wondered how she managed with classroom control. But once he had got to know her, he realised that under her gentle exterior there were nerves of steel. The word among the girls was, 'She's lovely but don't try playing her up. She'll fetch her stool.' Ceinwen had a stool on which she would stand to be at the same height as any recalcitrant girl to deal with her.

The only boys Ceinwen taught were in the sixth form. She was responsible for a short course for boys and girls heading for college or university. She found showing boys who towered over her how to boil an egg or make an omelette great fun and several of them fell in love with her, which is what Jackson did. He and Ceinwen began to go out to London theatres together, queueing under an umbrella in the rain for the cheap seats.

The two also went to church together. Arriving hand-in-hand to hear the great Will Sangster of Westminster on a Sunday evening, one of the stewards got to know them. 'Hullo', he would say, 'here come the two love birds.' Which is what they were. Jackson decided that the time had come to tell Ceinwen what had brought him to London. 'The devil tempted me and, like a fool, I fell into his clutches.' Ceinwen said, 'But Jesus taught that there is absolutely nothing for which we cannot be forgiven.' She came out with a slogan she had learned from life in London: 'Get over it, sunshine.'

After three years of teaching together, Ceinwen told Jackson she wanted to take him home to meet her parents. Her father was the Pastor at Criccieth Baptist Church and he and Jackson got on splendidly. The Revered Dewi Griffiths said, 'Ceinwen's letters are all about you. I assume you are serious about my beautiful daughter, otherwise I will call down lightning on your head.' Jackson grasped the opportunity. He replied, 'I think the Lord has brought us together. Please may I have her hand in marriage?'

Jackson rang home to speak to his father. He said, 'I know I have not yet been away five years but I want to come home and bring with me the girl I am going to marry. The Lord has brought us together and her father has given me her hand.' Jackson's parents found Ceinwen enchanting – his mother's word for anything of which she thoroughly approved. Marriage plans were discussed and Jackson explained that he and Ceinwen had found a house they could afford in the London suburb of Bromley. As the couple left and headed back to London, Emmanual Ubango said to his wife, 'Isn't it amazing how the Lord brings triumph out of disaster?' So it was that Black Dash, one time heartbroken olympic runner, lived to become a happy man.

THE LIFE OF KEN

Ken Bowden, born in Glossop, Derbyshire, became Borough Librarian in Bacup, Lancashire. He first made contact with the present author after reading some of his short stories. Although we have never met, we have since exchanged letters on a regular basis. Ken's letters have contained such a rich stream of anecdotes that publication of a selection has become inevitable if readers are not to be deprived of a valuable reading experience.

Peter Dawson and Ken Bowden were born respectively in 1933 and 1938 so we are now old codgers in our eighties with memories to share. We have both been Methodist preachers with evangelical tendencies most of our lives – Ken preached his first sermon as a young teenager in 1953 and his last in 2020. Ken is a life member of the Hymn Society. When only 19, he won a prize at the Glossop Youth Eisteddfod for writing a beautiful harvest hymn. Ken and his wife Ann celebrated their Golden Wedding in 2021 and her contribution to his lifestyle and sense of humour has obviously been significant.

Read on, dear reader, and be entertained, and also learn some history.

Our Glossop home cost £410 when purchased in 1940. My parents needed a £370 mortgage, which took fifteen years to pay off. We had no electricity, no fridge, no telephone, no central heating, no TV, yet I never felt deprived of anything that really mattered. But we did have an inside toilet and proper toilet paper. Not so Uncle Fred, who used newspapers cut up into squares. He reckoned the *Manchester Evening News* was very good for this purpose. When my mother, who was born in 1897, was a girl, it was her job to clean all the family shoes, for which she was paid a halfpenny a week.

When my dad was ill, little me wanted to get something to make him better. I toddled across the main road to Woolworth's and spent my penny on a Big Ben razor blade in a distinctive pictorial wrapper. How it was meant to make my dad better I have no idea.

Uncle Fred used to travel from Glossop to a wheelwright company in Manchester. One day he got the bus and, having no change, proffered a florin – a two shilling piece – for his twopenny fare. He apologized to the conductor, explaining that he had no coppers on him. 'You soon will have', said the conductor, and gave Fred twenty-two pennies change.

In 1945, when I was seven, I had to go into hospital to have my tonsils out. It was odd to be changing into my pyjamas at teatime in the summer, and positively upsetting when my parents went off and left me there. I was only in hospital two or three days. I've still got the bill, one pound five shillings, more than a quarter of dad's weekly income.

In the 1940s, sundry happenings took place to raise funds for our fighting forces. Three local mayors organized a concert and over a thousand folk enjoyed a reet good dowith the Halle Orchestra conducted by Sir Malcolm Sargent. It fell to one of the mayors, obviously a man with no great knowledge of the music scene, to move a vote of thanks. He did so by paying tribute to Sargeant Malcolm and his band. Sir Malcolm recalled the occasion when he later appeared on Desert Island Discs.

During the war, foodstuffs were in short supply. A certain uncle managed to find a banana for each of his nieces and nephews. He was stunned into amused speechlessness when they ate them, skin and all.

A highly significant day in my early life was 17 January 1944 when I began my primary education at Glossop Preparatory School (fees £5 per term) after running away from St Luke's School so often that the school medico advised my parents that something had frightened me and it would be in my best interests to switch to another school.

During August 1950, between leaving Glossop Preparatory School and starting at Manchester Grammar School, I was idly batting a ball along the pavement when it went under the railings into the nearby brook. I climbed the railings to retrieve my ball and fell into the brook. I must have screamed as a man from the nearby baker's shop came to my rescue and walked me home to where my mother was baking so the room was lovely and warm. No physical damage but I lost my cap as well as my ball.

Do you remember sweets called Refreshers? In 1954, at a rather wet school camp at Grasmere, four of us boys played cards for Refreshers. One evening I scooped the pool and put my winnings in one of my shoes overnight. By morning they had become a congealed mess.

Our school medico, Doctor Fisher, was at camp with us and one day went for a swim *au naturel*.

We had a poetry competition and the original draft of one entry read:

> We urinate against the wall,
> Which surely is not rude
> Compared with Doctor's latest feat:
> Swimming in the nude.

My dad took me on my first visit to London in May 1954, when I was fifteen. We lodged overnight in Bayswater. In default of being unable to lock our bedroom door, dad's solution was to shove an armchair under the door handle. Dad paid a local chap two shillings to show us the sights of London.

In terms of passing on the facts of life, my parents were never forthcoming on the subject. When one of my girl friends in Sunday School days got pregnant, all my mother would say was that a boy had sinned against her. No other details! But I came across a report in a newspaper in which a lad had fathered nine different babies but declined sterilization on the grounds that he might some day want to get married. Have such things changed for the better?

Did you do National Service? I've still got my card summoning me to Droylsden on 17 September 1957. I was graded D because of my flat feet.

During my career as a librarian, I found the following note as a bookmark:

> Keith, your sandwiches are under cloth on top of mangle, there's some beetroot or sauce, I've put tea in the teapot ready. If you go out, put some coal on fire and put guard in front <u>don't</u> stay out till lighting up time with the byke. Don't forget to lock the back door and go out the side and take the key with you. <u>Don't lose it.</u> If you do I'll kill you from your loving Dad.

Not long ago, I was due to pick up a passenger in connection with my voluntary driving job, but I was called away to play the organ at a funeral. I called County Cars Voluntary Driving to warn them that my passenger would have to wait, but my message did not get passed on. In the end, all was confusion and nobody was sure where I might be. Grandaughter Abigail (4) wondered what was happening. Her mum told her, 'Grandma's lost Poppa and we don't know where he is.' Twin Isabelle thought for a moment then said, 'Has grandma thought of looking upstairs?'

When Ann and I celebrated our Sapphire Wedding, she sent me a card which said: 'We have a strange and wonderful relationship. You are strange. I am wonderful.'

A CYCLING WORLD

Jack Brady ran a bike shop. Unmarried, he lived over it in a suite of rooms he redecorated throughout every three years. Everything was laid out in good order with no hint of untidiness. Each piece of furniture and each picture on the walls had its exact, unvarying place. He had a weekly cleaning rota which he carried out with great care, even down to polishing the door handles.

Jack's meticulous attention to the state of his home was down to his being extremely superstitious. He believed that anything out of place where he lived might signal some kind of disaster in his life. He smiled to see a famous tennis player who was always careful to line up his drink bottles with the labels pointing in the same direction. Jack thought that was why Rafael Nadal had won so many matches.

In his shop he stocked cycles of all kinds. There were some for children, many for daily use by adults who simply wanted to get around, also a range of racing bikes with multiple gears and refinements of every kind. Anyone wanting to compete at the local velodrome knew where to come for a racing bike.

In the centre of the shop, on a special platform, was the bike Jack had ridden in the Tour de France. In his prime, he took part for three years. His greatest achievement was winning a stage and earning a yellow jersey. In the window of his shop was a picture taken by the press of Jack on his bike, crouched over the handlebars, his head up, smiling at the camera. On a shelf he had constructed in the shop the many trophies he had won were on display.

Jack's ritual before a race was meticulous. While some competitors left their feet free on the pedals of their bikes, Jack attached his with straps. Sitting on his bike, he bent down and carefully tied each foot, then undid them and repeated the exercise twice more. He wanted, when asked why, to be sure he had done it properly.

He wore gloves to ride and had always to put the left one on first. When both were on, he clapped six times. Before mounting his bike, he would place one hand on the saddle and the other on the handlebars and say for all to hear, 'Here we go again. I'm depending on you, my friend,' then kissed the saddle. One experienced competitor would invite any newcomer to observe this ritual. 'Watch Jack Brady', he would say, 'he's the entertainment before we start.'

Thirty years after his days as a cycling champion, now aged 58, Jack was still as fit as a fiddle and reckoned to cover at least a hundred miles a week on his bike, either riding out into the country or at the velodrome, where he had honorary life membership. He was over six feet tall, lithe and muscular. He had a few girls friends but didn't think much of them. He rather crudely told his mates at the pub, 'With my arse on my saddle and my thighs pumping away as I race along, it's better than sex.'

One day a man came into his shop with a boy beside him. It was in the days of selective education and the man explained, 'Billy here just took his eleven-plus and I promised him a bicycle if he passed. Have you one that would be right for him?' It was just the sort of situation Jack liked, with someone about to start life on a bicycle.

He took the man and his boy over to the bikes for youngsters, saying to the boy, 'Congratulations. What a clever lad! Perhaps you will be able to ride your bike to school at the grammar.' After a bike had been chosen, Jack came out with his customary lecture. He addressed himself to the boy and asked him if he had a dog. 'Oh yes', came the eager reply, 'mum gave me and my sister one for Christmas. We call him Jumpy'. He paused, then added rather unnecessarily, 'He jumps about a lot.'

Jack said, with the boy's father nodding approvingly, 'I guess you were told that having a dog is for life, not just for Christmas. Well, it's the same with a bike. It needs to be cleaned and have its working parts oiled regularly. You need to learn how to maintain it. You need a repair kit for punctures. And you need to learn the rules of the road about riding a bicycle.' He gave the boy a leaflet he had written setting out the rules, which many cyclists were unaware of. As the father and son left the shop with the bicycle and everything else they needed, he said to Jack, 'Thank you very much for that lesson. I'll see that he sticks to it.'

One Sunday afternoon, Jack got on his bike and pedalled out into the Derbyshire countryside. The sun was shining and he felt that all was right with his world. A top-of-the-range Audi speeding at more than seventy came round a bend on the wrong side of the road and sent cyclist and bike high into the air. Jack lost his right leg above the knee and his left leg below. His despondency was awful to behold. He refused to consider having artificial legs, arguing that he still wouldn't be able to ride a bike at speed.

Jack sold his beloved shop and went to live in a bungalow. Day by day, he sat in the corner at the pub where of a picture of him in his cycling prime hung on the wall. He moped over glasses of beer, always ready to relate the grim tale of how he had lost his legs. His old mates gave up and steered clear of him.

One morning, Billy Stacey entered the pub and, seeing Jack, went over and greeted him exuberantly. 'Hey', he declared, 'you sold me my first bike after I passed the eleven plus. My dad says you turned me into a bike fanatic. Now I'm being considered for a team going for the Tour.'

Jack was nonplussed. 'What tour's that?' he asked. 'What tour?' said the young man, 'The Tour de France, you idiot. Have you forgotten what made you famous? I need your help in training. How about it? Come on, you started me on this road.'

'But look at me' Jack said, 'I'm in a wheelchair. The cycling world is closed to me now.' 'Rubbish', said the man Jack had introduced to the world of cycling. 'Get a couple of artificial legs and get back on yer bike. They can do wonders for people like you these days. Don't tell me you've forgotten what guts it took to ride the Tour. You've still got the guts, I'm sure, so use 'em.'

Some while later, inspired by what Billy Stacey had said to him, Jack confidently mounted a bike again. His expertly manufactured legs amazed him. He rode around the town, acknowledging those who remembered him. He became a leading figure in Discumgood, a charity for disabled people which helped them to come good. His good spirits and cheery dismissal of only having artificial legs raised the hopes and expectations of many who had little of either. He would tell them, 'Look, I'm the

Douglas Bader of the cycling world. He reached for the sky. I reach for my bike.'

He and Billy Stacy had become close. When Jack was learning to walk and ride again, Billy was there to encourage him. 'Just wait and see what you'll be able to do', he would say, adding, 'You know, dummy legs are like dogs. They're not just for Christmas, they're for life.'

A letter arrived telling Jack he was to be made an MBE in recognition of his charity work. He said to his mates in the pub, who no longer avoided him, 'I'm going to Buckingham Palace. Even in my cycling days, I never got as far as that when I had proper legs.' He laughed uproariously and his friends joined in.

MAKING FRIENDS

Rudolph the rhino was for the first time taking an interest in his appearance. Having reached rhinoceric adolescence, he had developed an interest in Rosalind, a young female rhinoceros. Standing knee deep in the water where rhinos and elephants came to drink, he looked down at the water. It was calm and acted as a mirror. Rudi did not like what he saw with a great ivory tusk sticking out of his face. He knew that men killed rhinos for their tusks but was ready to hand his over without any need for violence to make himself more attractive to the lovely Rosalind.

The rhino noticed a crocodile out of the corner of his eye. Clifford the croc was observing Rudi closely, but not with hostility. He had already had his main meal of the day when a young zebra that had wandered away from its mother and come too close to the water.

After being closely examined by the crocodile, Rudi asked somewhat aggressively, 'What are you looking at?' 'I'm just thinking that you are very ugly,' came the reply. 'Look who's talking!' Rudi responded, 'You are all great jaws.' He paused, choosing his words carefully. 'And you have a hideous hide.' The rhino was not one to mince his words and, being top of his English language class at the rhinacademy, he loved using alliteration, which they had just learned about. 'Yes', he said, 'you have a hideous hide, a horribly hideous hide.'

Rudi smiled with satisfaction at having put the crocodile in his place. Then he noticed that the croc was crying. 'What's the matter', he said, 'are you one of those who can dish it out but not take it. I can't stand creatures like that. The woods and plains are full of them. The lions are worst. They roar away, telling themselves they are rulers of the jungle, but my dad butted one of them with his huge tusk and it ran away. Right softies they are. Don't believe stories about the lion being king. Have you heard about a chap called Daniel being thrown into a lion's den and the lions being so terrified that they didn't dare touch him? At least that's how some theologians explain the story.' Rudi didn't actually know what a theologian was but he had heard talk about one when listening to his dad chatting to the minister at the Church of Rhinoceral Redemption where the family went some Sundays

'Theollyjeans', said Clifford, 'I thought they were sort of trousers worn by humins. My goodness, you're ever so well educated for a rhino, aren't you?'

'Theologians. The word is theologians, not theolly-jeans'. Rudi was pleased but a little embarrassed to have had his educated status recognized. He decided not to boast about being advised at the academy to try for a place at Rinobridge University when he reached the sixth form. Looking down at the water in which he stood, then lifting his eyes to the crocodile, he said, 'You know, we're both pretty ugly, aren't we? Let's be friends.' Which they firmly became.

Other animals shook their heads as they saw the two enjoying one another's company. 'I don't know what they are up to. It's unnatural,' said an observant giraffe. Observing things is easy if you are really tall. In the end, the two were called to attend a meeting of the jungle assembly. It operated in the same way as the ancient Greek polis, the city state.

In ancient Athens, every citizen was entitled to attend and speak. The polis was the first place to practice democracy, giving birth to the word politics. The jungle creatures knew none of this but had created their assembly in ignorance of it, which shows that animals aren't as daft as some folk think they are. The animals had elected Glenda Gorilla to preside over the assembly. She was not as fierce as males of her species but would stand no nonsense. She called the gathering to order as the chatter of the monkeys subsided.

'We are here today', she said, 'to invite a rhinoceros and a crocodile to explain their unnatural behaviour.' Rudi and his friend had agreed that he would speak for them. 'Ma'am', he said respectfully, 'we just like one another. We discovered this when we realized we had something in common, namely that we are both rather ugly.' 'You can say that again', interjected a disorderly young cheetah, who never could behave himself. Glenda banged her gavel and Rudi continued. 'Now we just like being together. We didn't mean to upset anyone.'

Benedict Bear indicated a wish to speak. Glenda nodded to him and he rose to his feet. 'Now we are going to get a lecture,' whispered Wilbur Wolf to his neighbour. Bennie, as the bear was known, lectured at the local FE college, the College of Furry Education. It had been established some years ago by a wealthy bear and admission was limited to hirsute creatures. 'We don't want any baldies here', said a furry jungle fox to a sleek cobra trying to get in, who slunk away. 'That took the sting out of him', laughed the fox's companion.

Benedict conducted a course at the college on PSHE, Peculiar Stuff Humins Enjoy. Some students said the most peculiar thing about the course was the lecturer, but they respected him for his immense knowledge of all things humin. He rose in his usual somewhat pompous manner in the assembly and began: 'As a matter of historical fact, what the two members arraigned before us today have done has been presaged.' 'What's that mean', whispered little

Millie Monkey to her big brother, who always knew everything. 'It means it's been predicted, forecast, suggested before.'

'Long ago', said Bennie, 'among the humins there was someone named Eyes Higher. We think it was at a time when the eyes of a few humins, who were clever at seeing what was going to happen in future, might have been on top of their heads. We think they were called puffits, or something like that. This chap Eyes Higher wrote a book in which he said the time would come when there would be peace in the world. One sign of it would be animals getting together and being nice to one another.' Bennie bent down and picked up a book. He lifted it over his head and said dramatically, 'I have what Eyes Higher wrote right here. Listen':

The wolf will settle down with the lamb.
The leopard will lie down with the little goat.
Children will be able to play with snakes.
Animals will no longer try to hurt or destroy
one another.

'What a load of nonsense', shouted the lion. 'No it's not', said an antelope timorously, 'It would be lovely.' 'I'll deal with you later', growled the lion. 'You'll have to catch me first', she said bravely. She had outrun the lion before. Glenda banged her gavel furiously. 'I will not have you threaten one another in this assembly. The next one who does it will be conducted out. Now, Benedict, I think you have more to say.'

He had. He always had, as his students knew. 'Well', he said, 'we have to understand that Eyes Higher was speaking *metaphorically*.' He emphasized the word. He knew some of his hearers would have no idea what it meant but he liked using long words. He explained. 'Eyes Higher was saying that peace would one day come to the earth. The image of animals at peace with one another meant humins would be at peace with one another one day.'

Glenda spoke. 'It seems to me that the rhino and the croc are ahead of the rest of us. Maybe we should all try to make peace with one another.' 'But how will we survive if we can't eat one another?' asked Terry Tiger. 'Perhaps we should all become vegetarians', said a voice from the back of the assembly, laughing.

Although Rudi and Clifford had survived their interrogation, it seemed to make no immediate difference to the way the animals treated one another, except that the lion and the antelope had been seen chatting together happily as they left the assembly.

HIS WORDS A MEMORIAL

Jimmy Buckstone hadn't thought of joining the RAF but his father, a flight sergeant in technical wing at RAF Burnaby and, after thirty years service maintaining one of Britain's fighter squadrons, had more or less made it inevitable, although never having suggested it to his son.

Jimmy was a bright lad who was doing well at grammar school, despite preferring the sports field to the classroom. He was confident of getting three not-bad A Levels but had no interest in further study after that. Rugby in the winter and cricket in the summer had taken precedence over academic swotting at school and he had no wish to enter undergraduate life.

When Jimmy had gone for his interview with Mr Boggis, the careers master at school, in year twelve – what they used to call the lower sixth – Boggy was surprised that the young man had no interest in going to university. 'No sir', Jimmy had asserted, 'that's not for me. I want to get on with my life; see the world; do something ...' he paused, '... do something that *matters*.'

'I see' responded Boggy, 'well is there any tradition in your family of service that matters; anyone in the caring professions; anyone in the business field creating things we need to survive; anyone in the civil service; anyone defending us from our enemies?' The careers master was pleased with himself for putting things so lucidly.

Richard Boggis had been doing the careers job for many years and many boys bored him with their banal ambitions. He rather took to this Buckstone boy.

Jimmy, as his name implied, bucked up his ideas in response to the teacher's prompting. 'My father's in the RAF', he said, 'keeping one of our Tornado squadrons in the air. I guess he's defending us from our enemies. I never thought of it like that before.' 'Well, give it some thought', said the teacher, 'you would get a commission and see the world. Service life can be a good life for those who take to it. And you would certainly be doing something that matters.'

While preparing for his A Levels, Jimmy applied to join the RAF, to the great delight of his father. 'Just think', said his dad, 'I could end up having to salute you.' 'You could practice by saluting me', said mum. 'That'll be the day', said Flight Sergeant Buckstone, laughing.

Some years later, Squadron Leader James Buckstone led 161 Tornado Squadron with panache.

That was why he was chosen for a six month tour at RAF Mauripur in Pakistan, an RAF staging post near Karachi. The purpose of the posting had been clearly spelled out to him by an Air Vice Marshal responsible for fighter deployment.

Buckstone was told, 'Now that the days of the Raj are long gone, India has descended into chaos, falling apart into two nations, Hindus in India, Muslims in Pakistan. They are so busy hating one another that they have no thought for the strategic importance of the sub-continent for us. We need to show them we are still around and that our base at Mauripur is still of critical importance. It is our staging post between Britain and the Far East.'

The man who had chosen Buckstone for the task in hand went on: 'We need to show Pakistan, and the world of the Middle East, that we are here for good. Your job is to fly the flag; get your squadron in the air and perform; have the local citizenry open-mouthed with amazement; invite the local bigwigs to a dining-in night; make the Mauripur show the talk of the town.'

Jimmy's father had retired from the RAF. His pride in his son was enormous but he was uneasy when he learned of Jimmy's posting. He said to his wife, 'I hope he'll be alright out there. Some of them don't like us you know.' His wife Amy replied, opening her response with words she often a had to use in dealing with her husband these days about all sorts of things. 'You've forgotten what you used to say.' Flight Sergeant Buckstone, retired, no longer had a reliable memory. His wife went on: 'You told everybody the RAF existed to defend us from those who don't like us and, by God, you were up for it. Anyway, you know what Jimmy's like. He'll charm the whiskers off the locals.'

Six Tornados of 161 Squadron rocketed across the sky in a tight V formation, climbed vertically, turned upside down in a beautiful arc at the top of the climb and levelled off after completing a perfect circle. They dropped their noses for a vertical descent, still in tight formation. Their frightening plunge to earth caused a supersonic boom as they breached the sound barrier. They levelled off and thundered off across the desert stretching away from the city of Karachi below, whose citizens had watched the performance open-mouthed. Lieutenant Crosby, on duty as controller in Mauripur Tower, said, 'Bloody marvellous. The Red Arrows in their toy aircraft have nothing on this lot. I don't know how they do it. Yes, I do. It's Buckie. He's a magician.'

One of the pilots in 161 was asked what it was like to have Buckie leading the squadron. Flying Officer Danny Plant said, 'He's brilliant at making you believe that what he wants you to do is just what you have always wanted to do. That applies to a triple roll at high speed in the air or wearing your cap straight walking about the station. I think it's called charisma. I'd fly with him into the mouth of hell.'

The three massive bombs that exploded at the Paradise Cinema in Karachi killed hundreds and wounded thousands. The rescue operation was frantic and, like the customary management of the city's affairs, chaotic. Hearing of what had happened, Squadron Leader Buckstone called his men together and said, 'Come on. We must go and help. We must show them we care about them and their city.'

Three jeeps from Mauripur airfield pulled up by the remains of the Paradise. The huge mountain of rubble that had once been the cinematic pride of Karachi had people all over it moving broken slabs of concrete and shattered bricks aside as they searched for survivors. At one point, three men had opened up a cavern into the heart of the wreckage. They stood over it, wary of clambering into the hole they had made.

Squadron Leader Buckstone came up in company with Flying Officer Plant. They were not in uniform but fatigues, ready for some heavy work, but one of the men who had opened up the pile of wreckage recognized the Squadron Leader from a visit he had made to Mauripur. 'Hooray!' he declaimed, 'The RAF have arrived. We don't know what to do now we've made a hole.'

Jimmy said, 'You've done a great job already. Now we must go in there and get people out.' 'But it might collapse', came the reply. The man his colleagues called Buckie was adamant: 'We'll have to take a chance on that. This is the moment for some real heroics. Come one Danny.'

The two flyers climbed into the hole. Within half an hour, they had found, pulled out and passed to the men who had dug the hole, two young women and an elderly man. All of them were dusty, bleeding, but still very much alive.

The Squadron Leader and his colleagues were dirty and exhausted, but Buckie was for going back into the hole one more time. Danny Plant was dubious. There had been creaks and groans from the wreckage as they had climbed out. But Danny followed his boss back into the hole. Suddenly, the whole edifice began to collapse. Danny withdrew just in time but the man he admired above all others was gone. Quietly, Flying Officer Plant whispered to himself, 'I said I would fly with him into the mouth of hell, and I did.'

Some years later, Squadron Leader Plant became an effective leader of men, though less charismatic than the man under whom he had once served. Everyone knew that he had flown with Buckie, who was something of a legend among fighter pilots. Dahlia, as Plant was affectionately known in the officers' mess at RAF Manston, was a quieter version of his exemplar, but gave the same answer as him when asked what was the secret of effective leadership: 'You have to make those you lead believe that what you want them to do is what they have always wanted to do.'

Plant offered the same advice in his speech when invited back to his old school to present the prizes at prizegiving. Jack Ainsley, in only his second year teaching at the school, thought to himself that getting his year nine maths set to do their homework involved persuading them they wanted to do it. He thought he would get better at it in time and hear fewer groans when telling his pupils, 'You know you really want to do it.'

The Headmaster immediately added the speaker's words to his collection of memorable quotations. 'I guess', he told his deputy, 'it sums up what we are up to in the classroom.' Hearing this, Brian Crouch, who taught British Constitution in the lower sixth, said, 'It's what every Prime Minister has to do in handling his cabinet. Persuading them they want to do what he has in mind is a struggle. And every PM has the same problem with senior civil servants. Margaret Thatcher complained that the civil service was riddled with champagne socialists who had no intention of carrying out her policies. Their masterful command of delaying tactics made her furious.'

Squadron Leader Plant was unaware that his advocacy of his one-time leader's advice had hit home so powerfully. He felt sure that Buckie would have been pleased to learn that his recipe for effective leadership might apply to teaching the young and governing the nation. The influence of his words was an important part of Squadron Leader Jimmy Buckstone's memorial.

HATING SUNDAYS

'I hate Sundays'. Sue Grey's words shocked her hearers, two old school friends who met with her for lunch every now and again. Sue explained. 'Mike is off most of the day conducting services, leaving me to handle the kids, then, at the end of the day, he has the youth group here for a sandwich supper, prepared by me, of course, and a questions-about-God session that goes on and on. Then, would you believe it, Mike puts on his jazz records to unwind. I hate Sundays.'

'Well', said her friend Julie, 'you know how surprised we were when you married a Reverend. We thought you were much too lively to get involved in all that boring church stuff.' She paused and added, 'Mind you, we all thought Mike was a real stunner.' 'He still is', said Sue ruefully, 'when he decides to give me a bit of attention, which is not often.'

'The trouble with men', asserted Midge, the third of the trio, 'is that they can only concentrate on one thing at a time. Mine is great in the garden when he is having one of his flower crazes. Last summer, after we'd been to a local flower show, he bought a greenhouse and grew some magnificent dahlias. This year, I don't think he's been out to the greenhouse once. He's joined the local badminton club to keep fit.'

The three young women met every few weeks to have lunch together at a local pub and share their joys and sorrows – mostly joys because all three had secure marriages and happy families. Perhaps that was why they were able to talk openly about their lives at home and exchange advice on how to handle any difficulties.

Sue said, 'Jackie wants to go away for a weekend with her mates to the Westbury Music Festival. She says all the top bands will be there. She sounds very sensible about it. They aim to stay at a local B&B rather than camp at the festival site where drugs might be pushed.

Mike says OK. She's sixteen and we can trust her. But he's worried about what some of the church folk will say, especially as Jackie will want to be quite open about it. A feisty girl, she says Mrs Burley, bastion of the old guard at church, needs to realise that not all teenagers are wild and irresponsible, even if they wear jeans with rips in them.' The girl was very proud of her own pair, given to her after her father had asked what she would like for her birthday and found her answer, as he explained to his wife, challenging.

Julie said: 'Good for Jackie. She'll have a great time at the festival and come back as lovely as before. Sue, you and Mike have done a fine job raising her, and never mind what some church folk think. After all, the worst that can happen is that Mike will be kicked out of the Methodist Ministry. What a great story that will be in the *Methodist Recorder*, not to mention the tabloids. I can see Jackie and her dad being interviewed on TV. What a kick up the backside that will be for the old guard.'

'Stop it,' said Midge, laughing, 'you'll get Sue worried. If Mike ends up unemployed, what will he do? I know, him and my Ted can open a garden stall selling dahlias. Actually', she went on, 'I have a serious problem at the moment.' The others turned to her, concerned. She was not the sort of person to see a difficulty unless it was significant. 'Our Jimmy, who is now seventeen, has been excluded for telling a teacher he was a racist. We have to go and see the Head.'

'That doesn't sound like Jimmy', said Sue, 'he's a very polite, mild-mannered sort of lad.' 'Yes', said his mother, 'but he speaks up if he feels an injustice is being done. There's a new teacher at the school who was doing General Studies with the lower sixth. They were doing the recent history of the Middle East and he said Hamas was justified in wanting to wipe out Israel.'

'The teacher said the Jews had stolen the land of Palestine from its original inhabitants. God had promised the Jews a land of milk and honey so, after the Exodus, they walked in and snatched it. When Britain made the mistake of recognizing the state of Israel after the Second World War, it created a whole load of trouble.'

Midge went on: 'Jimmy says Hannah Ginsberg, who sits behind him, was in tears so he spoke up and said the teacher's account of history was biased. He said saying the Jews should be eliminated, as Hamas does, is surely racist. His close friend Jake Levin backed him up. Jake said, "Sir, Jimmy is right. Israel is wrong to be extending its territory today, but the Arabs asked for it when they invaded Israel. Surely there can only be peace in the Middle East when the Palestinians accept Israel's right to exist?"'

But the teacher would have none of it. 'Look', he said, 'everybody knows that the Jews are an avaricious, power-seeking tribe that take over the economy of any place they are found and dominate its affairs. The world would be a better place without them.' 'Sir', responded Jake, 'Jimmy is right. You're a racist.'

The teacher exploded, 'You two, get out of my classroom now. I'm going to report you to the headmaster.' 'Please do', said Jake as the young men left the room, 'because we will be reporting you. Come on, Hannah, join the revolution.' The sobbing girl followed the boys out.

Richard Stone, the Headmaster, was astonished. Grey and Levin were two of the school's brightest prospects academically, and leading figures on the sports field. Neither had ever been in any kind of trouble before. When the new teacher, Roger Tracey, explained what had happened, Richard Stone found him unconvincing. His insistence that he was only trying to promote debate, uttered as he shifted uneasily from one foot to the other, left the Headmaster in little doubt about what to do. His deputy agreed. 'I think', said Geoffrey Brock, who had been at Bickley Grammar School for thirty years, 'Mr Tracey's time here is going to be brief.' Given a written warning as to his future conduct, he chose to resign.

The next time Jimmy's mother met her friends Sue and Julie, she had a tale to tell. Jimmy's exclusion from school had been lifted without the need for his parents to attend upon the Headmaster. Ted said he was pleased he wasn't going to have to put an exercise book down his trousers. 'But', she said, 'Jimmy has become very quiet and thoughtful. He says the incident – that's what he calls it – the incident has made him realize the impossibility of peace in the Middle East and anywhere else. He says we live in a world divided by terrifying hatreds.' She said, 'He sounds so ... mature. My little boy has gone.' Sue said, 'Well, the world may be full of hatred but I don't hate anyone. I just hate Sundays.'

THE MUSIC TEACHER

Alan Bird was an excellent teacher of woodwind instruments at Greenford Grammar School for Boys. One of his clarinet pupils had reached the final of the BBC Young Musician of the Year competition. As well as the clarinet, Alan had pupils learning the flute and the oboe. One unusually tall boy asked to play the bassoon. 'Sir', he said, 'I want an instrument as big as me or I'll look silly.' Alan's contribution to the school's reputation for having a fine orchestra was greatly appreciated by Richard Hevey, the head of music at the school.

The biggest challenge Richard Hevey faced each year was rehearsing the hymns for Founder's Day with both the boys and the associated girls' school nearby. Both schools had originally been established by a rich silk merchant, who also financed the building of the local Anglican Church, Saint Matthew's, in the eighteenth century. It was the custom each year for both schools to go together to a service at the church to give thanks for the founder of the church and the two schools. In preparation, Richard Hevey would practice the hymns with the boys one morning after assembly. On the previous morning he would have gone down to the girls' school to do the same.

Getting seven hundred boys to behave themselves and take hymn practice seriously was a problem, Richard Hevey being limited in the area of disciplinary control. That being so, the deputy head, adopting a dour countenance, would sit on the stage to oversee proceedings with other senior staff sitting round the hall. On one occasion, when the boys' performance was not good enough to please the head of music, he proclaimed, 'Come on you boys. Let's have more effort. Put a bit of body into it like the girls do.' The deputy head's face went puce as he repressed his laughter. The event was never forgotten and often rehearsed by those who had witnessed it.

Richard spoke highly of Alan Bird in the staff room. 'He knows how to inspire boys who have a potential for musical success inside them. We have boys in this school who are brilliant academically but have no musical ability at all. On the other hand, we have boys who don't shine in the classroom but have great musical potential.' 'Oh, come off it', said Jack Blower, geographer and staff room cynic, who regarded all boys as his natural enemies, 'Don't tell me the bottom stream have a potential for anything but messing about. They are all as thick as two short planks.'

He went on, 'Take that boy John Soper. In my subject, he still can't read an ordnance survey map after three years.' 'But', responded the head of music, 'he's a star of the school orchestra. He plays the oboe as if born to it. Haven't you ever heard him play? He did the oboe solo part when the orchestra played Mozart at prizegiving last year.' 'No', said Jack Blower, 'I wasn't really listening. I don't go much on music unless it's the Beatles. I couldn't tell you the difference between an oboe and a sticky toffee pudding.'

But Alan Bird's days as a highly successful instrumental teacher were numbered as the local education authority looked for ways of cutting costs. 'If young people want to learn to play a musical instrument, their parents must pay for private tuition', asserted the chairman of the education committee.

The head of music at Greenford Grammar was downcast at losing the services of his three instrumental teachers, and especially at having to tell Alan bird he could not retain him. The Headmaster argued with county hall, pointing out that parents would not be able to pay for their sons to be taught privately. 'We have some boys from very deprived homes here', he asserted, 'and there's no way they will be willing or able to pay for private tuition of any kind. When a boy reached the final of Young Musician of the Year, the local authority was glad to celebrate his success and claim part of the credit.

Well, the boy's father had a greengrocery shop and struggled to pay for his son's school uniform.'

But the Headmaster's pleas achieved nothing. Those who had been instrumental teachers at the school had to look elsewhere to earn a living. 'There's nothing for it', said Alan Bird to his wife, 'but classroom teaching. I had a hard time of it on teaching practice when I was training to teach, but we've got to eat.' His wife laughed. 'I would do almost anything for you except starve.'

The man who had achieved wonders with clarinet, flute, oboe and bassoon with boys of musical bent applied to teach music and history, his subsidiary subject at college, at a grammar school for boys and girls. His experience as an instrumental specialist in a boys' grammar school had not equipped him for what lay ahead.

Classes applied the usual tests on the newcomer to the staff to discover the extent of his classroom control. Alan Bird's first history lesson with a class of fourteen-year-olds set the tone. The topic was Tudor England. Mention of the king's several marriages had one girl asking, 'Sir, are you married?' Naively, the teacher replied, 'Yes, I am'. 'Sir,' asked another girl, 'is it as good as it was at first?' 'Be quiet', replied the teacher, nervously, 'we are here to study history.' A boy chimed in: 'But, sir, didn't Henry VIII wanting to have it good with Ann Boleyn change history?'

Steadily the calling out of provocative questions increased as the teacher lost control. The noise from the classroom became so great that the teacher next door came in to quieten things down. At the end of the lesson, as the class left the room, the girl who had set the game of tease-the-new-teacher in motion by asking if he was married paused at the teacher's desk and said quietly, 'Sir, we like you really.' Walking away, she waggled her hips provocatively.

Teaching music was even more difficult. Alan had been delighted to see that the classroom allocated to him had a piano. However, when he turned away from a class to play it in the course of teaching, paper aeroplanes were fired in his direction, and sometimes more dangerous missiles. When a steel ruler hit him in the back of the head he lost his temper and ranted at the whole class.

What annoyed him most was the way in which, in moving about the corridors, boys and girls would make tweeting noises as they passed him, making a joke of his name. Often, he entered the staff room in a boiling rage. 'The boys and girls in this school have no manners and are completely out of control', he ranted. 'Those you teach may be so', said the head of science pompously, 'but you have to ask yourself why. We teachers, you know, create our own conditions in which to practice education.' 'Yes', said Jenny Ogbourn, biology, 'it's like with dogs. There aren't any naughty dogs, only owners who have not trained them properly.' Jenny had a labrador who was the light of her life.

Alan Bird knew he was in trouble when it was made known that Ofsted were coming to inspect the school. He told his wife, 'I could give the Headmaster a list of pupils who ought to be excluded for the duration of the inspection. If they are here, we will fail.' He paused and added, 'Well, for sure, I will.' But, in the event, his disastrous performance was a blessing. The music inspector was a kindly man who showed real understanding of Alan's position.

'You can't enjoy teaching here', he said. 'You aren't really a classroom teacher, are you? I guess you are one more instrumentalist caught in the trap of education cuts. That lesson in the room with keyboards was positively dangerous.'

The inspector was referring to a lesson Alan had attempted to conduct in which he was teaching a class to play music on electronic keyboards. He had started by telling them that many pop groups had them, hoping that would make them enthusiastic, but their enthusiasm for playing about on the keyboards made teaching impossible. The racket could be heard across several classrooms.

Having lost control, Alan went to the corner of the room where a long pole rested. He took it, went to the middle of the room and swung the pole to strike a beam in the ceiling. It immediately switched off all the electrics and brought a short period of astonished silence. 'One of these days', Alan shouted at the class, 'when you make me do that, someone is going to get electrocuted.' 'Yes, sir', declared one of the boys, 'you, sir!' The laughter was uproarious.

'When you went and fetched the pole', said the inspector, 'I thought you were going to batter the lot of them. You must find another post, before you cause a disaster. Let me try and help you. You need to work as an instrumentalist in the private sector where local authority economics don't apply, or maybe in a further education college with a music tradition. I will give you a list of some in this area. You must do some knocking on doors with your excellent record at your previous school in your hand.'

So it came about that Alan Bird secured a post at the Lattery School of Music, so named in honour of the great James Lattery, conductor of the Birmingham Symphony Orchestra in days gone by. The school was a private college for young people who wanted lives in the world of music. As a woodwind teacher there, Alan was overwhelmed by the ecstatic enthusiasm of students for making music. They could never get enough of it and Alan found himself happily exhausted when he got home each day. His wife said, 'Sweetheart, you are a changed man. Thank God for that school inspection.' It was not a verdict often heard when it came to the Ofsted inspection system. 'Yes', said her husband, 'I think it saved my life.'